P   98368
Arnold
 Quick, quack, quick!

A NOTE TO PARENTS

When your children are ready to "step into reading," giving them the right books is as crucial as giving them the right food to eat. **Step into Reading Books** present exciting stories and information reinforced with lively, colorful illustrations that make learning to read fun, satisfying, and worthwhile. They are priced so that acquiring an entire library of them is affordable. And they are beginning readers with a difference—they're written on five levels.

Early Step into Reading Books are designed for brand-new readers, with large type and only one or two lines of very simple text per page. **Step 1 Books** feature the same easy-to-read type as the Early Step into Reading Books, but with more words per page. **Step 2 Books** are both longer and slightly more difficult, while **Step 3 Books** introduce readers to paragraphs and fully developed plot lines. **Step 4 Books** offer exciting nonfiction for the increasingly independent reader.

The grade levels assigned to the five steps—preschool through kindergarten for the Early Books, preschool through grade 1 for Step 1, grades 1 through 3 for Step 2, grades 2 through 3 for Step 3, and grades 2 through 4 for Step 4—are intended only as guides. Some children move through all five steps very rapidly; others climb the steps over a period of several years. Either way, these books will help your child "step into reading" in style!

For my son Calvin–
the original Quack
–M. A.

Copyright © 1996 by Marsha Arnold. Illustrations copyright © 1996 by Lisa
McCue. All rights reserved under International and Pan-American Copyright
Conventions. Published in the United States by Random House, Inc., New York,
and simultaneously in Canada by Random House of Canada Limited, Toronto.

Library of Congress Cataloging-in-Publication Data: Arnold, Marsha Diane.
Quick, Quack, quick! / by Marsha Arnold ; illustrated by Lisa McCue.
p.   cm. — (Step into reading. Step 1 book)
SUMMARY: A very slow duckling saves his family during a crisis.
ISBN 0-679-87243-4 (trade) — ISBN 0-679-97243-9 (lib. bdg.)
[1. Ducks—Fiction.   2. Speed—Fiction.]   I. McCue, Lisa, ill.   II. Title.
III. Series.   PZ7.A7363Qu   1996   [E]—dc20   94-38054

Manufactured in the United States of America   10 9 8 7 6 5 4 3 2 1

STEP INTO READING is a trademark of Random House, Inc.

Step into Reading™

Quick, Quack, Quick!

A Step 1 Book

by Marsha Arnold
illustrated by Lisa McCue

Random House 🏠 New York

4

Into the barnyard
came a duck
and her ducklings.

All but one.

He stopped

to visit the baby pigs.

"Quick, Quack, quick!"
his mama called.

Quack started to follow.
Then he saw a butterfly.

"Quick, Quack, quick!"
his mama called.
"Quick, or the chickens
will eat all the corn."

Quack pecked
at a kernel of corn.
Then he heard the birds.

"Quick, Quack, quick!"
his mama called.
"To the pond.
It's time to swim."

Quack ate berries
along the path
to the pond.

"Quick, Quack, quick!"
his mama called.
"Into the water."

But instead

Quack played games

around a hollow log.

He danced on the log.

He hid in the log.

"Peep, peep,"

Quack said into the log.

"QUACK! QUACK!"

came out the other end.

Finally Quack jumped
into the water.

"Tails up,"
said his mama.

As the ducklings swam,
the sky changed
from blue to pink.

It was time to go home.

"Quick, Quack, quick!"

his mama called.

"Back to the barnyard.
Soon it will be dark
and Cat will go hunting."

21

Quack started to follow.
Then he saw
more berries.

One berry.

Two.

Three berries.

Four.

"Quick, Quack, quick!"
his mama called
from far away.
Quack had to stand
on top of the hollow log
to see his family.

But what was that behind them?

"Mama, Mama, look out!"
Quack called.
But she was
too far away to hear.

Quack jumped
off the log.
"Peep! Peep!" he said
into the log.

Quack's mama
heard a loud
QUACK! QUACK!
She turned around
and saw Cat!

QUACK

QUACK

Mama Duck
snapped her beak
and charged at Cat.

Cat ran away,
far, far away.
Quack's family
was saved!

"Dearest Quack,"
his mama said,
"for once I am glad
you were <u>not</u> quick!"

African-American Heroes

Chris Rock

Stephen Feinstein

Enslow Elementary
an imprint of
Enslow Publishers, Inc.
40 Industrial Road
Box 398
Berkeley Heights, NJ 07922
USA
http://www.enslow.com

Words to Know

Bed-Stuy (sty)—A nickname for Bedford-Stuyvesant (STY-vuh-sunt), a neighborhood in Brooklyn.

comedian (cuh-MEE-dee-un)—Someone whose job it is to tell jokes and make people laugh.

comedy club—A club in which comedians perform.

housing projects—Apartment houses for poor people to live in.

open-mike night—A night when a club invites people up to the stage to perform a comedy act or a song.

strict—Having strong rules that must be followed.

Enslow Elementary, an imprint of Enslow Publishers, Inc.

Enslow Elementary® is a registered trademark of Enslow Publishers, Inc.

Copyright © 2008 by Enslow Publishers, Inc.

Library of Congress Cataloging-in-Publication Data
Feinstein, Stephen.
    Chris Rock / Stephen Feinstein.
       p. cm. — (African-American heroes)
    Includes index.
    Summary: "Elementary biography of comedian Chris Rock discussing his childhood, early career, and his rise as one of America's most famous comedians"—Provided by publisher.
    ISBN-13: 978-0-7660-2894-4
    ISBN-10: 0-7660-2894-1
    1. Rock, Chris—Juvenile literature. 2. Comedians—United States—Biography. 3. African American comedians—United States—Biography. I. Title.
    PN2287.R717F45 2009
    792.702'8092—dc22
    [B]   2007044916
Printed in the United States of America

10 9 8 7 6 5 4 3 2 1

To Our Readers: We have done our best to make sure all Internet Addresses in this book were active and appropriate when we went to press. However, the author and the publisher have no control over and assume no liability for the material available on those Internet sites or on links to other Web sites. Any comments or suggestions can be sent by e-mail to comments@enslow.com or to the address on the back cover.

♻ Enslow Publishers, Inc. is committed to printing our books on recycled paper. The paper in every book contains between 10% to 30% post-consumer waste (PCW). The cover board on the outside of each book contains 100% PCW. Our goal is to do our part to help young people and the environment too!

Every effort has been made to locate all copyright holders of material used in this book. If any errors or omissions have occurred, corrections will be made in future editions.

Illustration Credits: AP/Wide World: pp. 1, 2, 3, 5, 9, 15, 16, 18, 19, 21, back cover; BedStuyGateway: pp. 3, 7; Everett Collection: pp. 11, 17; Getty Images: pp. 13, 20; Photos.com: p. 12.

Cover Illustration: Everett Collection.

JUN 2008

Contents

Chapter 1

Growing Up in Brooklyn

Chris Rock was born in Andrews, South Carolina, on February 7, 1966. When his parents, Julius and Rose, were growing up, life in the South was very hard. African Americans did not have the same rights as white people. In the 1960s, things were changing for the better. But Julius and Rose wanted the best for their children. So in 1972, when Chris was six, Julius and Rose moved the family up north to Brooklyn in New York City.

Chris Rock grew up to be one of the funniest comedians in America.

Chris and his five brothers and one sister grew up in a part of Brooklyn called Bedford-Stuyvesant. The people there called the area **Bed-Stuy**. Chris and his family lived on a nice street. But they were only three blocks from the **housing projects**, where there were drug dealers and gangs. Julius and Rose taught their children that it was important to choose their friends carefully.

Chris's parents were hard-working people. Rose was a teacher, and Julius drove a delivery truck. Rose and Julius were **strict** parents. They told their children that hard work was the only way to find success in life.

This is Bed-Stuy, the neighborhood where Chris grew up.

Chapter 2

Making People Laugh

By the time he was six, Chris saw that he could make people laugh. He liked to tell jokes and funny stories. Chris dreamed of becoming a **comedian** when he grew up.

Rose and Julius believed that the schools in Bed-Stuy were not as good as the schools in white neighborhoods. So when Chris was in the second grade, they sent him by bus to P.S. 22. All of the other kids in the school were white. Many of them did not like African Americans. They teased Chris and called him bad names. They picked on him and beat him up.

Chris likes to make funny faces that make people laugh.

James Madison High School was even worse. The white kids were very mean to Chris. He tried to get through each day without getting beat up. Chris wanted to tell jokes at school, but he had no friends. Back at home, Chris still got his family to laugh at his jokes.

Chapter 3

Chris Becomes a Stand-up Comedian

Chris was very unhappy at school. In 1983, after finishing the tenth grade, he dropped out of school. He worked at one job after another. The only thing he enjoyed was telling jokes to the other workers. What Chris really wanted was to work as a comedian in a **comedy club**. There he could perform on a stage and make the whole audience laugh.

One day in 1985, Chris went to Radio City Music Hall to see his favorite comedian, Eddie Murphy. While Chris was waiting in line, an item in his newspaper caught his eye. It said that the comedy club Catch a Rising Star was having an **open-mike night**. This could be the big chance he had been waiting for!

Eddie Murphy was Chris's favorite comedian. He did the voice of Donkey in the *Shrek* movies.

At an open-mike night for comedians, people who think they are funny get up on stage and do their act. When the audience at Catch a Rising Star heard Chris, they laughed loud

and hard. Chris performed often at that comedy club. His dream of becoming a comedian was coming true.

This is Chris when he was starting out as a stand-up comedian.

Chapter 4

"The Funniest Man in America"

One night in 1986, Chris was performing at a club called the Comic Strip. Eddie Murphy was in the audience. He liked what he heard so much that he gave Chris a small role in his movie *Beverly Hills Cop II*.

In 1990, Chris tried out for NBC's television show *Saturday Night Live*, and he got a part. For the next three years, he appeared every Saturday on the late-night comedy show.

This was the cast of *Saturday Night Live*, a comedy TV show. Chris joined the show in 1990.

Chris went on to make comedy specials for cable TV. He also appeared in many more movies. One of his favorites was *Madagascar*. He did the voice for the character of Marty the Zebra. He also did the voice of the title character in the movie *Osmosis Jones*.

Chris doing a comedy special on TV.

In the movie *Madagascar*, Chris did the voice of the zebra.

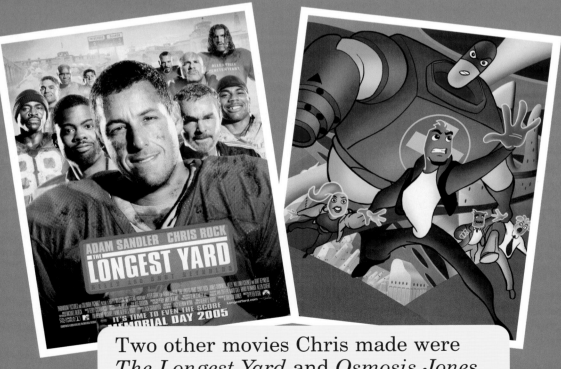

Two other movies Chris made were *The Longest Yard* and *Osmosis Jones*.

In 1996, Chris married Malaak Compton. Their first daughter, Lola Simone, was born six years later. Their second daughter, Zahra Savannah, was born in 2004.

Chris, Malaak, and their daughters, Lola and Zahra.

Chris won many awards for his comedy.

Meanwhile, Chris was winning awards for his work and had become a big star. *Time* magazine called Chris the "funniest man in America."

Chris with Tyler James Williams, who plays the part of the young Chris on the TV show *Everybody Hates Chris*.

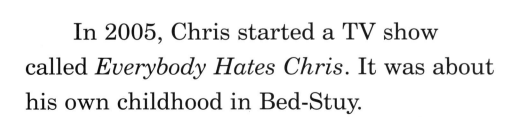

In 2005, Chris started a TV show called *Everybody Hates Chris*. It was about his own childhood in Bed-Stuy.

Chris Rock had come a long way from Bed-Stuy. He had worked hard to become a success.

Timeline

1966—Chris Rock is born in Andrews, South Carolina, on February 7.

1972—Chris's family moves to the Bedford-Stuyvesant section of Brooklyn, New York.

1983—Chris drops out of school after finishing the tenth grade.

1985—Chris performs at an open-mike night at the comedy club Catch a Rising Star.

1986—Eddie Murphy sees Chris at the Comic Strip, a comedy club.

1990—Chris joins the cast of the TV show *Saturday Night Live*.

1996—Chris marries Malaak Compton.

2002—Chris and Malaak's first daughter, Lola Simone, is born.

2004—Chris and Malaak's second daughter, Zahra Savannah, is born.

2005—Chris starts the TV show *Everybody Hates Chris*.

Learn More

Books

Bany-Winters, Lisa. *Funny Bones: Comedy Games and Activities for Kids*. Chicago: Chicago Review Press, 2002.

Blue, Rose, and Corinne J. Naden. *Chris Rock*. Philadelphia: Chelsea House Publishers, 2000.

Todd, Anne M. *Chris Rock: Comedian and Actor*. New York: Chelsea House Publishers, 2006.

Web Sites

***Everybody Hates Chris* Web site**
<http://www.cwtv.com/shows/everybody_hates_chris>

***Madagascar* Web site**
<http://www.madagascar-themovie.com>

Index